CW01096171

Provinzen

Translated from German

Provinces
Tabea Steiner

Translated from German by
Jozef van der Voort

First published by Strangers Press, Norwich, 2022
part of UEA Publishing Project

All rights reserved
Author © Tabea Steiner, 2022
Translator © Jozef van der Voort, 2022

Printed by
Swallowtail, Norwich

Series editors
Nathan Hamilton & Lucy Rand

Editorial assistance
Lily Alden, Erin Maniatopoulou and Emma Seager

Proofread by
Senica Maltese

Cover design and typesetting
Glen Robinson (aka GRRR.UK)

Design Copyright © Glen Robinson, 2022

The rights of Tabea Steiner to be identified as the author and
Jozef van der Voort to be identified as the translator of this
work have been asserted in accordance with the Copyright,
Designs and Patents Act, 1988. This booklet is sold subject to
the condition that it shall not, by way of trade or otherwise, be
lent, resold, hired out, stored in a retrieval system, or otherwise
circulated without the publisher's prior consent in any form
of binding or cover other than that in which it is published
and without a similar condition including this condition being
imposed on the subsequent purchaser.

ISBN: 978-1-913861-49-0

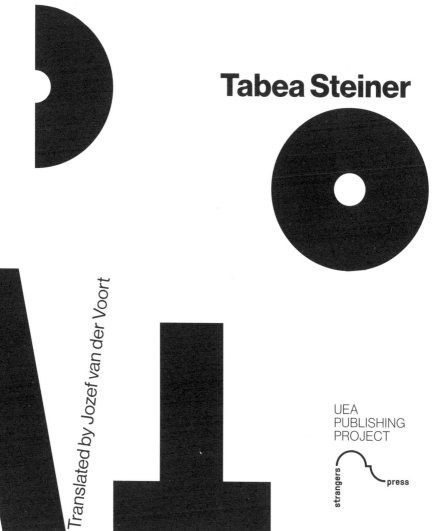

Tabea Steiner

Translated by Jozef van der Voort

UEA
PUBLISHING
PROJECT

strangers press

PROVINCES CONTENTS

WINDOWS ON THE WORLD

THE FLAT I MOVED INTO SIX MONTHS ago can be accessed from the front or the back. To get to the front door, I go past a Japanese and an Italian restaurant, a cupcake shop, a Portuguese-run news kiosk, the Salvation Army street kitchen and a store selling Ghanaian products. The route to the back door takes me through a low vehicle entrance and across a courtyard where children often play football until late at night. Sounds and smells drift from the surrounding blocks; a Swiss flag hangs in one window. The building I live in backs on to a Spanish restaurant – one of the smartest venues in town, people say.

Mine is a bright apartment on the ground floor with windows on three sides. The reception is bad, so I tend to sit by the living room window when I'm on the phone. Outside, people walk past with shopping bags and vegetables; cars are parked, kids whizz around on skateboards. When I open the window, people can look into the flat from the street. There's something oddly intimate about making eye contact with a passer-by who also happens to be on the phone.

Even as a child, I used to love sitting by the window and looking out at the main road that cut through the countryside in front of our home. The lilac bush that grew between the house and the road harboured a bird feeder during the winter. Our cat used to crouch beneath it and whenever a bird landed, I would be on tenterhooks. I'd never have forgiven it for eating a bird, but I never shooed it away either.

One cold Sunday morning when I opened the windows of my flat to let in some fresh air, I saw a man. He approached slowly, in a wide arc, as if to postpone his arrival. Eventually he came face to face with me and asked for money to buy food for his children. The only thing open nearby was the Italian patisserie. With the usual ambivalence, I handed him some of the cash I had. Later I saw him carrying a large brioche, which is all he could have bought at the bakery with what I gave him.

During my first rainstorm, I watched as the large wheelie bins at the front of the building were blown into the road. Slowly they drifted out, one after another, weaving back and forth, forcing cars to swerve. After the storm, when calm was restored, I noticed that the boy and girl who'd sat together on the wall beside my building every evening all summer long had disappeared. They'd talked for hours on end, never smoking, never kissing.

There haven't been any break-ins since I moved here, but I know that a computer was stolen from this apartment on a Saturday morning years ago. It's that time of day when the streets are at their emptiest; the clubbers have gone home, the residents are asleep. Somebody must have climbed in through the kitchen window, crossed the apartment and then climbed back out of the living room.

The kitchen is narrow; there's no room for a table. I often use the windowsill instead, though it's a squeeze for two. When visitors come, we eat in the lounge under the nice lamp or sit in the sofa nook over an apéro.

From the kitchen window, you can see the old bikes in the courtyard; the expensive ones are kept in the basement. At the far end, the bins are lined up at the back of the Spanish restaurant.

People come here in search of leftovers; when they find something, they sometimes look around before leaning against the wall to eat it. First thing every morning, the waiters tip crates of empty bottles into the glass bin. The restaurant doesn't list prices on its wine menu.

Two perfectly round box plants adorn the restaurant entrance; apéros are served on the forecourt in summer. The only way from the restaurant to the rear courtyard is via the smokers' lounge. Men in suits stand around between our old bikes and their expensive cars; they stub cigars out underfoot, drink, and soon notice the bike bells. The valet parks their cars out back for them and, at the end of the long evenings, the vehicles wind their way round to the front again. It reminds me of the time I picked up a screwdriver when I was little and used it to peel a sinuous spiral of paint from the side of our car. Before they head home, some of the guests come out into the courtyard, unbutton their suit trousers and piddle first-rate liqueurs against the wall.

On Christmas Day, there was salmon for breakfast. A man walked past the kitchen window. He looked inside – hesitant at first, then curious. I waved; he waved back and walked on, only to reappear a moment later. I paused before opening up. Was there a vacant flat in the building, he inquired. I didn't know, but pointed at the block across the way; maybe he meant to ask over there?

The only way to the laundry room is down some steps from the rear courtyard. Even now, on certain days, you come across people on the way down who are smoking from tin foil, giving off a vinegary odour; very occasionally you see them injecting too. Other venues have been opened for them on the outskirts of this city, which was until recently notorious for its open drugs scene. They apologise, step aside, and by the time you come back for your clothes they're gone. Often by the time you start the machine.

When I go up to the roof terrace, I can look into the flats above the Spanish restaurant. On the first floor there's often a man standing by the window in his vest. I can also see him from my kitchen window – sometimes without the vest. But whether I'm in the kitchen or on the roof, I can't tell if he can see me. Maybe it's the windows that make his vest look dirty, or maybe it's my eyes; right on top of one of the smartest venues in town, there's social housing.

Shortly before I struck out to live in a big city for the first time, I read about how after the fall of Ceaușescu and the closure of Romania's state-run orphanages, hundreds of abandoned children had taken up residence in Bucharest's sewers, where they then grew up and in some cases had children of their own. In Las Vegas there are people who have to painstakingly redecorate all over again whenever the rain washes their decor out of the storm drains they call home. And in New York too people live in the subway tunnels, while the city's urban canyons are flooded with daylight because an early planning regulation states that skyscrapers in Manhattan must always taper upwards.

The fourth floor is home to a man with a bird on his shoulder. Music plays from somewhere or other, day in, day out. From the roof, I look out over one of the most expensive cities in the world. Sounds drift up to me from every street; there is sunlight in abundance.

Just now I was drinking coffee in the kitchen. Two very young but fully grown men crossed the courtyard carrying buckets. We noticed each other, exchanged nods. Then I watched them throw open a window on the first floor. The only way to get to these apartments is through the side entrance; the dense scrawl of names on the doorbell panel tells you how many separate units there really are. The man in the vest briefly appeared behind the two young men before vanishing again, and they both gingerly donned their gloves. One of them leaned out and spat into the courtyard in front of my window. He looked at me, gave an apologetic shrug and set about his work. By the time the men left the building again through the service entrance, my coffee had gone cold. I watched them head off and wondered whether the lilac bush was still there, and why it is that birds still don't eat cats.

55 SIENNA STREET

PLANNING OUR TRIP TO ARMENIA, WE'D opted for a con‐
necting flight with a long layover in Warsaw because the tickets
were cheaper. I didn't know much about Armenia beyond a handful
of facts: that the national church has its own pope; that the Berlin–
Baghdad railway could only be built with the forced labour of
countless Armenians; and that during the genocide, people were
driven into the desert without food on various occasions in order to
starve them to death, children included.

We took a while to find Sienna Street as we went the wrong way
from the train station at first. Every few seconds, a Mercedes-Benz
logo flashed at us between the new glass skyscrapers and the
broad, pompous Soviet-era edifices. The three-pointed star revolved
in endless circles, scattering sunlight far over the city.

55 Sienna Street is situated in a quiet spot next to a fast
food stand, which is closed on Sundays. Kids were playing in the
courtyard, but the gate was locked. We were in two minds about
whether to speak to them, but eventually one spotted us, paused
and dashed off, before quickly returning accompanied by an older
child. The two of them sized us up before pressing the door release
button and paying us no further attention.

The first thing I noticed on entering the yard was a framed photo
of a pope on the wall of a first-floor flat. This pope, whom I can only
think of now in connection with the popemobile and his lonely death
on TV, was staring in the direction of the fast food stand, though this
lay hidden behind a wall that must have been twenty feet long and ten
feet high. He was gazing out benevolently over this space, it seemed
to me, as if he were looking back at us from his sunlit province
through a telescope that compressed the years into a minuscule lens.

✳

A few weeks prior to this journey, Claude Lanzmann had died, and
his death had reminded me that I'd once watched *Shoah* in a single
day — as if so much could be condensed into nine hours, and as if
those nine hours could be compressed into one day.

In the final scene of the film, a man talks about how he smuggled
himself into the Warsaw Ghetto through sewer tunnels in order to
carry messages back and forth. On his last such errand, he found
the ghetto utterly deserted. He describes how he stood alone in a
courtyard and believed himself to be the last human on earth, left
behind because he had been travelling through the underworld
while everyone else was deported.

This man had left the ghetto and been tracked down one way or
another by Lanzmann, to whom he finally told his story of solitude.

After the Berlin Wall came down in 1989, the Americans set
out for 55 Sienna Street to retrieve a fragment from the wall of
the Warsaw Ghetto, which had once stretched for several miles.
A plaque marking the spot where the bricks were chipped out

states that they are now on display in the Holocaust Museum in Washington DC.

The Americans also brought takeaway stands that churn out endless chains of fast food.

We stood for a moment in front of this scrap of wall, which you can also examine in America, and then we left the courtyard, waving our thanks to the children. An enamelled sign on the house front of 55 Sienna Street shows a photo of a small throng of people formed in line and bearing arms, ready for the Warsaw Ghetto Uprising of 19 April 1943.

High up on the building across the road, an eye-catching billboard for the fast fashion brand Etam featured the slogan 'The French Liberté', with a model who looked gaunt in a way that was almost passé. Spotlights had been installed to illuminate this gargantuan poster at night; it must have been visible from all over town.

After dark, back when the ghetto wall was still several miles long, these same streets and lanes would have been flooded with light during curfew, with skeletal figures flitting here and there through the squares and alleyways, sealed off inside the walls.

We walked back to the train station, a building whose location and importance have shifted and altered multiple times over the course of the twentieth century. This time we found our bearings straight away, bought tickets back to the airport, located the departure lounge, boarded our flight and landed a few hours later in Yerevan. In the dead of night, we set foot in Armenia, that small, hot, fertile country.

HEIDI MAKES USE OF
WHAT SHE HAS LEARNED

MY GRANDFATHER GREW UP IN AN orphanage and spent his boyhood dreaming of life on the land. He married a young widow whose late husband had bequeathed her a splendid farm in the winegrowing region to the north of Zurich. After just a few years the woman left him; she took their seven-year-old twins and slipped away under hazy circumstances. He stormed and raged, but she didn't return; the animals lowed more piteously by the day and, because he stubbornly refused to look after them until she came back, a deadline was issued and the farm was sequestered.

For decades afterwards, he traded manual labour for lodgings in a barely insulated shack where no one could bother him – and when people tried, they soon learned better.

Those who still remembered him after so many years had to rub their eyes in amazement when he replied to a letter informing him that one of his daughters had herself given birth to twins. It's to this change of heart that I owe my memories of the man, who always smelled faintly of stale walnuts, who came and went as he pleased in his red Volvo – his second home – without ever giving us notice, and who only took out health insurance when the government forced him to. On our seventh birthday, he pulled up in his car, opened the rear door and lifted out two lambs, which my sister and I raised by bottle.

※

In Johanna Spyri's novel, we learn that Heidi's grandfather the Alm-Uncle frittered away his family farm in Domleschg when he was young and moved away to Italy, where he served in the army and was rumoured to have killed a man in Naples. On returning with his son, Tobias, he moved into a lonely mountain hut perched high above the village. Tobias died young, his wife followed soon after, and their young daughter went to live with an aunt.

One evening, while the old hermit was sitting by his hut and looking down on the valley, he saw two figures climbing the slope and reached for his field glass. Peering more closely, he recognised the aunt, who was dolled up and decked with feathers the likes of which he had only ever seen in Milan. Beside her was the little girl, who had a head of curly hair the likes of which he had only ever seen in Naples. The child kept stopping and stamping her foot and her aunt kept tugging at her arm, until eventually she broke free and squatted on the ground. The Alm-Uncle watched through his glass as the stately lady stalked towards him without once looking back at the girl. Then he got up, walked into his hut, bolted the door and closed the shutters against the ascending past.

After a few carefree years in the mountains, Heidi and the Alm-Uncle received another visit from the aunt, who had resolved to fetch the girl against her will and take her to a foreign land. Heidi received an education, and by the time she returned, she could read and write and put two and two together.

During her time abroad, Heidi had been plagued by home-sickness and bad dreams. Night after night, perhaps, she'd been haunted by visions of her friend Peter's blind grandmother dying; that might explain why she'd started setting aside bread rolls for the old woman. When she was finally permitted to go home, Heidi found the Alm much as she'd left it: the goats, young Peter, the blind grandmother, it was all still there.

The Alm-Uncle was still the same old Alm-Uncle too. And now that Heidi had learned to read and write, she read her grandfather the story of the swineherd who squandered his whole inheritance and who wasn't even suffered to eat from a trough with the pigs, until he finally resolved to do the only thing left to him: he kicked the trough over, dusted himself down and set out for home. After many days and nights of walking, he eventually arrived where only the dogs recognised him at first. The son asked his father's forgiveness – I have sinned in the eyes of God and men – and the father had the son bathed, dressed and perfumed and bade his servants roast the fatted calf until it was golden brown. Understandably, the other son, who'd stayed at home to help his father, complained at such a feast being made for one who had frittered his share away on whores.

Heidi had no fortune to squander in the first place, and the thought that in faraway Frankfurt she hoarded stale bread rolls in her wardrobe for Peter's blind grandmother – well, it breaks your heart. It's remarkable that she prevailed on the Alm-Uncle to rejoin village life and to at least spend winters in the valley so she could go to school. And nobody could reproach her for lecturing her grandfather about the Prodigal Son and prompting him to take her to church – even though that meant facing the pastor, who had been the first to tell him that the girl needed to go to school. In the end, Heidi even convinced Peter the goatherd of the use of reading and writing and checked his homework for him.

And yet when Clara came to the Swiss Alps on a cure, the sole reason she learned to walk again was because the jealous Peter pushed her wheelchair down the mountain out of spite.

For my part, I was not an especially wayward child. I remember a time when some acquaintances of my parents invited us to lunch and I sat at the very bottom of a long table, far away from the grown-ups and next to Lorenz. Lorenz was seven years older than me and already owned a whole flock of sheep, while I had only a lamb. I mainly liked Lorenz because he had a rabbit called Fritz, whom he'd trained to pee with surprising force at anyone who came too near. But Lorenz ignored me all through lunch while I tried to talk to him about sheep farming, and so I pinched him hard on the leg.

These days, I live in a heated apartment, I have health insurance and I work with children who come to school on their afternoons off for lessons in German as a second language. Although many of them speak very good German, they make their way across town in all weathers to sit in a windowless classroom — a converted boiler room — with their immaculate exercise books on their desks and their bike helmets on the floor. And on the rare occasion that they want to skip this voluntary class on their only free afternoon of the week, they always ask for permission in advance.

In the classroom, I put up a poster with a cartoon showing crowds of holidaymakers by a mountain lake and I ask the children to point things out and arrange them into grammatically correct sentences. Hands shoot into the air. I can see a Swiss person, one girl says, but amid all the tourists playing football and eating ice cream, I can't make out anyone obviously Swiss. Up there, she says, standing on tiptoe by the poster to point the Swiss person out to everyone: in the top-left corner — the place on the page where you start reading and writing in Roman script — a tiny boat is flying a Swiss flag as it sails across the lake.

Sometimes the children also have to come in after school to help their parents understand what I tell them. On one such evening, a boy tells his mother off for signing a form from right to left in her own script. And a father with high expectations for his daughter tells me of his own schooldays when he had to cycle to the senior school in the neighbouring village, and how he dropped out after two days because it was too windy. Then, like an actor who thinks the cameras are off, he adds that all that remains of his bike now is a molten mass in the backyard, incinerated by a barrel bomb.

These children do not speak of nightmares or of homesickness, and most of them don't know why their parents brought them to this foreign land. One boy tells me there are just too many flies under the toilet lid at home. Most of the kids don't know who their grandparents are. Maybe they sense they'll fare better here than the strangers they see in photos at home.

One girl has stopped attending the voluntary German lessons. She hadn't stood out in her regular classes until year five, when she'd developed the singular tic of stamping her feet, clicking her fingers, slapping the desk and bumping her elbows against her knees, only to return studiously to her sums as if nothing had happened. Understandably, the other children, who wanted to solve their problems in conscientious silence, had complained because they couldn't write neatly with the desk wobbling under them. And understandably, the other children had also complained when the girl who couldn't stop stamping and snapping her fingers got a desk of her own while everyone else had to share.

Another solution was found for her in another school at the other end of town after long discussions revealed that she'd never stopped adding up on her fingers, so that when she came up against more challenging problems, it took more than just her hands: she had to put her whole self into it.

EXPOSURES

THE SLIDE PROJECTOR HAD BEEN SWITCHED OFF; the lights in the hall were about to turn on. The cone of light in which dust particles had danced was already extinguished; yet it lingered on the retina, its negative hovering darkly over the darkness. For a brief moment, the projector could be heard whispering as it cooled down. Then the lights came on and movement crept into the audience.

Inside a projector of this kind, a small lever pushes each slide to one side so that the next can fall in front of the bulb. Between images, the screen is briefly flooded with light, and the same happens at the end of the film too. Sometimes two slides drop into view simultaneously.

The word 'film' here refers to the oblong yellow box holding the slides. The number of slides is the same as the number of photos on a roll of film, which, once finished, automatically winds back into the camera with a loud whirring noise. The roll is then packed up in a canister and sent off to be developed, and a few weeks later an oblong package arrives.

The film that had been projected was a slow-moving one with a commentary on every single image – some brief, some in-depth. The slides spoke for themselves but were expounded upon all the same; the person providing the commentary had made a selection and chosen the order. The same person also determined the speed by pressing the switch that slotted the next slide into place, even though projectors had long since been invented that could cycle through the pictures automatically at regular intervals.

I was little and I often sat in the front row for these slide shows. Sometimes I would lie on my front and peer up at the screen from the carpet, my hands propped against my cheeks, watching people appear, magnified, dark-skinned. There they would stand, exposed to the audience, sometimes with arched backs and protruding bellies, unaware that at this very moment they were being studied by a small group of people in a little auditorium somewhere in the middle of Europe. Unaware too that the missionary who had photographed them was standing beside the screen. The congregation had sent him out into the world, but now he was on holiday and he had returned to talk about his work – about how these magnified people on the screen beside him had found their way to the light. They lived in another time zone, one that was dark while ours was bright.

There was no television or radio in my parents' house. I would lie on the carpet and listen raptly, soaking up the missionaries' explanations and those grainy images from a strange, faraway world, and it would feel to me as if the cords that held together the innards of my own world were being pulled taut inside that small, dark room – as if they were being drawn into an inextricable knot. Around this time, I learned years later, other children my age were watching the first war ever to be broadcast live on television.

The missionaries would store the finished rolls of film in the coolest place they could find, and on their holidays brought them back home to Europe to be developed in order to report on their work in the field — on what had been done with the donations. The people in the pictures appeared individually and in groups, adults and children. Sometimes they posed in traditional clothing such as grass skirts, with spears in their hands and painted markings on their faces and bodies.

Behind them stood their homes: circular huts arranged around a village square, high-rise houses woven into the treetops. The landscape featured too, along with animals, birds of paradise, butterflies, a handful of chickens and a multitude of pigs. When the 'brown folk', as the missionaries called them, held feasts at Christmas or Easter, they would dig a hole in the ground, line it with red hot stones and cover these with banana fronds before adding leafy greens, rice, sweet potatoes and pork and leaving it all to cook for several hours. This dish was called mumu, the missionaries told us, and was also prepared for 'heathen' festivals.

Other photographs showed classes from both weekday and Sunday school with laughing boys in neat shirts gathered around their light-skinned teacher.

※

Here at my desk, where I am writing down my memories, twelve mouse clicks are all it takes to zoom so far out on Google Earth that the entire globe is displayed before me. When I rotate it slightly with my cursor, I see Australia at the bottom right, and directly above it the islands on which these missionaries set up camp. I can move the Google globe to make these islands the centre of the world. I can also flip it upside down, or spin it to show nothing but water.

Papua New Guinea is surrounded by legions of islands; the country itself is divided from Indonesia by a perpendicular line that is laden with history. Beyond this line, I knew, lay mountains and forest, but these were outside the missionaries' field. It was a magical frontier, much like Lake Constance, which I grew up very close to. Beyond it, I knew, lay Germany — a place we never visited where the sky seemed different, more precipitous somehow, or like the delicate fabric of the heavenly canopy that kept us safe. (But from what?)

The missionaries rarely showed photographs of white people. Or perhaps I've simply forgotten that there were photographs of white people; I don't know how to check, or whom to ask for permission to look through the thousands of pictures I saw in my childhood, which were all in a sense similar, viewed from below, lying on my front.

We mainly saw the 'brown folk', as they were called. I can't recall a single photograph of a white missionary taken by an indigenous person.

In the early days of colonialism, when photography was yet to be invented, imperial masters would commission paintings of themselves being borne aloft through exotic locales by indigenous servants, their faces turned aside to enjoy the scenery. Yet our missionaries removed themselves from the frame; they stole away from view.

☀

Family photos were taken with the help of the self-timer. We would line ourselves up in a row while my father set up the camera, arranged us all in the right position and finally pressed the button. Then he had a few brief seconds to dash back and insert himself into the picture.

On Sunday afternoons, the screen would be set up in the living room to view the slides together. There too I would lie on my front on the carpet and look at family photos together with my family, as a group, working in the meadows, the apple orchards and strawberry fields and on holiday in the Swiss mountains. Recent history brought into the light.

In retrospect, the moments of my childhood that flashed up on that screen in two dimensions, blurry and doubled, seem to lie much further back in the past than my childhood itself — even though at the time I could clearly remember the events captured in those slides. In retrospect, those Sunday afternoons themselves feel like time-lapse exposures: moments merged into light and memory, in which fleeting snapshots of my childhood paraded before me in an endless loop.

✳

The mission whose fieldwork was explained to us came into being at a time when colonialism had largely ceded the field to aid work. As early as the sixteenth century, missionaries followed merchants out into the world and saw themselves as the salt of the earth while globalisation ran its course through the trade in exotic spices.

The missionaries played their part in colonial exploitation, subjection and destruction, and the fact that colonialism and photography developed at the same moment in human history leaves me deeply discomposed.

✳

The indigenous women did not appear on-screen in traditional clothing; instead they wore t-shirts and skirts that had been collected during the congregation's donation drives. The missionaries never showed the women's bare breasts, but simply told us how they would nurse their children until the age of five for practical reasons, so they would always have food for them. They carried their children on their backs and their water containers on their heads, and they wore cast-off skirts from the women in the hall.

Sometimes we saw pictures of pot-bellied children, not so much due to hunger as to their arched backs. Sometimes they had gaping, vivid wounds, and in one case − this stayed with me − a hacked-off foot. Yet the diseases and plagues that missionaries carried with them all over the world, bringing death to innumerable indigenous people who were hopelessly exposed to them, and against which the missionaries' own medicines had no effect, went unmentioned.

✳

In its early days, photography was seen as blasphemous, and Walter Benjamin wrote of how he didn't dare to look people portrayed in daguerreotypes in the eye because he was afraid they would meet his gaze. Similarly Stygian qualities were ascribed to television at first too.

One of the missionaries explained how the brown folk were afraid of the camera because they thought it would carry off their souls. That made it all the more necessary to preach the good news to them – to redeem them from the blood feuds between the different tribes as much as from their belief in spirits.

As a child, that made sense to me, in much the same way as what I was told about football made sense. At the 1994 World Cup, the Colombian team was eliminated during the group stage due to an own goal by Andrés Escobar and as a result, on his return to Colombia, Escobar was shot dead. During another match in the same tournament, two opposing sides wanted to wear a black kit. Yet the coin toss decided not only which team could play in black, but also who would ultimately prevail. The prince of darkness, I was informed, had queered the pitch in an extraordinarily manifest way.

※

The village where I grew up was briefly home to a woman of whom I know neither what she did before she arrived nor where she later moved. All I know is that she lived in an apartment in the attic of a house that belonged to the parents of one of my school friends, and that she was black. I sometimes went to play at my friend's house and one time the woman invited us upstairs for a slice of cake and a glass of coke. She wore a colourful headscarf along with a pair of jeans – an item of clothing that nobody wore at home. Once we had finished our food and drink, she put on some music and showed us how to dance to it.

I burst into tears. The woman tried to console me, to hold me, but I ran down the stairs and all the way home, where I was held, reassured and praised for resisting temptation. At home, dancing was considered heathen.

※

One of the missionaries told us – with regret – that he had once been to the cinema. During the interval there had been an advert for Coca-Cola and for a fraction of a second a naked woman had appeared on-screen. It had been so brief that the image merely prickled the subconscious without being visible to the human eye, but he saw her all the same.

When I think back to the slide shows, I don't remember them as colour photos but as sepia-toned, as if soaked in Coca-Cola. Yet colour television was already widespread by then and has been broadcasting increasingly strident reports about globalisation ever since — something I didn't hear much of as a child.

At the end of the slide show, once the projector had been switched off and the lights in the hall had come on, the missionary stood by the door and bid a personal farewell to each and every member of the congregation. Beside him stood the collection box: a small plinth topped with a figure of a kneeling brown boy who nodded steadily to thank us for the donations we pushed into the slot in his neck.

SOCIAL FREEZING
APRIL 2020

MY MOTHER CALLED ME AT 3:47 P.M. on 11 September 2018. I looked at the display, then back at my screen. I had another three and a half pages to go if I wanted to stay on track with the edits on my debut novel, which meant another two hours' work.

I called her back at 6:30 p.m. It had taken me a little longer to finish because I somehow knew this wouldn't be a good conversation.

That it would be about my father was obvious. But what was happening, how serious it was, whether he was even still alive — that, I didn't know.

He was in intensive care. They'd taken him straight to St. Gallen because the cantonal hospital was the nearest of Switzerland's ten certified stroke units. But we didn't know any more than that. He was awake only for brief moments; he was restless and hallucinating.

The following day I had an appointment at the fertility clinic. The doctor was a few years younger than me and during my first visit a few weeks earlier had greeted me with the words, so you want to have a baby? Well, you're in the right place. That strikingly rhythmic turn of phrase still echoes in my ears to this day. He bade me sit down, look at a chart, go through his work with him — his analysis of all those samples and tests. The odds are slim, he said — not impossible, but slim — that you will ever have a child.

31

I wanted to cry. It's not so bad, he said, we have lots of options. I got up and left without having examined a single one of those options; in just a few hours it felt like the semantic field of the word 'life' had ossified.

✳

Towards the end of 2018, my father underwent multiple operations and lay in a long coma and I often came to sit or stand at his bedside for a few hours at a stretch. He lay there breathing, but not independently; the machine breathed for him, the machine beeped and hummed and puffed for him, it lived for him, and everywhere I looked there were curves, lights, screens with graphs, heart rate, brain activity, who knows what else? All I know is that you flinch every time something happens on those screens that you don't understand – in other words, constantly.

My father lay there just as my sister had done many years earlier when she came down with meningitis and the inflammation spread to her brain; it was doubtful that she would survive and the doctors were certain she would suffer lasting damage if she did. She lay there puffing at the machine for weeks on end too, but I was with her when she woke up and the first word she said was 'wolf'.

While my father hovered between life and death in the autumn of 2018, my friend's first book came into the world and I went to the launch. It was a lovely evening; there was a white dog there and lots of people too – familiar faces, friends of friends and just plain friends. Some of them asked me how I was doing. Good, I said; Are you sure? they asked. Yes, just my bag is a little heavy.

I said my goodbyes early, walked home along the river and cried – in part because I couldn't just tell those friends, friends of friends and familiar faces that I wasn't OK. Nobody would have taken it badly, nobody would have asked stupid questions; there are no stupid questions. I walked home alone and thought back to the time at school long before my sister lay in hospital with encephalitis when I didn't answer my friends after they asked me what was the matter. We saw each other every day, but for two long weeks I didn't tell them that my brother had cancer, that it had already metastasised and they'd had to operate straight away, that same evening. I was convinced – and I even realised this at the time – that none of it would be true if I didn't say it out loud. But there was no doubting the truth during the years that followed, in which my brother was subjected to a steady drumbeat of chemotherapy sessions at the University Hospital in Zurich and his hair fell out and grew back over and over again, alternately straight and in tight curls. These days his hair is straight.

Nor was there any doubting the tumour that appeared five and a half years later, or the tumour they found in autumn 2019, in late October or early November, shortly before the winner of the Swiss Book Prize was announced – and with my novel, which I had somehow managed to finish writing, on the shortlist. Yet that rotten tumour proved benign in the end and only needed to be surgically removed.

And life in the autumn of 2019 went on regardless, much like it had towards the end of summer 2018, and all the while my mind fell back to those months and years when I was still a child, and my brother was still a child too, and my sister was starting to blossom into a young woman when, two weeks before she finished school, she fell. It was a complex fracture that dislocated the ball of her hip and confined her to bed for weeks on end. The bed-rest made her first chubby, then puffy; her skin turned red and her hair began to fall out in round patches. She was taken to see specialists at the cantonal hospital in St. Gallen where after long months she was diagnosed with lupus, an autoimmune disease, and until the age of twenty-five she spent much of her time in hospital.

I can't recall how much time passed – I could find out, but it was just childhood time – between my sister's accident and my father's earlier stay in hospital; all I can really remember are the many walks I took with him after he came home, just the two of us, with him holding an IV pole and me at his side, though later on he didn't need the IV. Either way, I always had to walk very slowly because otherwise I would have left him behind when I wanted to keep an eye on him. I only learned years later that these surgical procedures – and there must have been several – were the delayed outcome of a birth defect: my father had come into the world without a bowel outlet and while still an infant, with access only to medical technology that was nowhere near as developed as what we have today, he had undergone countless operations.

What I did already know back then was that when my father was four, his own father had died of polio, and during his illness, his life and that of a young boy had both depended on access to the sole available ventilator. They'd decided to give it to the family man; they'd had to make a choice, and there was no way they could have known that my father's father – my grandfather – still wouldn't survive. If that boy had lived, he would be a few years older than my father is today, and who knows? Perhaps they would sit together in the canteen of the care home where my father spends every afternoon with the friends he's made there.

And that's all I can tell you. Right now, I can't bring myself to write about all the familiar and not-so-familiar faces in the faith community I grew up in who made it known that diseases were a punishment from God. Yet I'm scared for my sister, whose body produces antibodies that don't defend against infections, but target her own tissues and cells instead. I'm always scared for her, but all the more so now because she works on an emergency ward.

And I feel a little embarrassed because I realised yesterday that I've been getting stitches while running because I hold my breath as I pass other people.

But fear and embarrassment get us nowhere. Not much will get us anywhere right now besides staying at home, waiting it out, gathering knowledge. One of the most important moments of my life was when I read Susan Sontag's observation that the instinctive belief cancer can only be kept at bay if it isn't put into words is itself almost a symptom of being close to someone with cancer.

Ever since I read that I understand a little better why there are some things I can't really talk about — why my insides set like concrete when someone I know is diagnosed with cancer. And I think I understand why I only wanted to cry and couldn't just cry in that doctor's surgery, surrounded by posters of embryos blooming on the walls.

We cannot control life with knowledge; we cannot — and I am certain of this — control life. But we can find words that give names to our fears, that give shape to what is diffuse. We can write these things down and we can talk about them. We can tell other people — familiar faces, friends of friends and just plain friends — what is bringing us down, and this is a little easier when the right words are available to us. And yes, sometimes I feel sad that I don't have a child, and no, that doesn't mean I'm unhappy with my life.

I know there are times when we simply can't speak. We are human. But by now I know it brings us closer together to say things out loud, and that no familiar faces, no friends of friends and above all none of my friends will ask stupid questions.

What we are experiencing now, in the spring of 2020, is a situation of stress beyond compare, and there is nothing we need more than to be close to other people. Social distancing is the catchphrase of the moment, but for me the term keeps morphing into another: social freezing. Yet social freezing is already taken; I need to find another linguistic expression for this appalling absence of my friends. Social freezing refers to the precautionary preservation of unfertilised eggs for no medical reason — a technique originally developed for young women who were about to undergo chemotherapy.

THE SKY OVER ZURICH

AT THE FOOT OF THE ALPS... past the peaks of Pizol and
Vorab; over Glarus and the Kaltbrunner Riet, that scrap of remnant
marshland; then skirting the Nuolener Ried bird sanctuary (ugh,
puh-lease!) and swooping down over the Frauenwinkel wetland for
a glimpse of the Siberian irises and marsh gentians (they say even
lapwings breed here)... at the foot of the Alps, nestled between
lateral and terminal moraines, lies Lake Zurich.

So many glacial remains; here Wädenswil town, there the
Sihlwald with its bears and wolf packs, then a sharp turn at
Kilchberg to sail over the water, ignoring the botanical garden, the
Gessner garden too with its traditional healing plants – but ah,
the opera house, time to rise again and catch a glimpse of distant
Munich. Long ago, all this lay under ice.

A dome: the university. Looks interesting, but only from afar; too many footnotes.[1] No one needs tourist information these days. The Marriott, empty; no kids in the Dynamo youth centre. Eventually the river widens; time for a bath – here, now, yes – but look, a mouse, and over there a beetle. Feathers itching again; a jab of the beak extracts a flea.

Just upstream, the big train station; they've channelled the water under the rails. Sure to end badly, but none of our business. A pleasant air current wafts from that direction – an invitation to take wing again – but goodness, what are they up to in the passport office? No matter; here, catch the turning down Dammstrasse. The tulip tree, empty. Perfect. Pigeons are fine but no crows, please, crows are no good. Cautiously hop several tree-stops along to the horse chestnut; a few days ago, the leaves were still tucked inside their tiny finger-buds. But wait – this must be the window. There she is. Perched by the glass. Not looking out.

NOTES

[1] 25 March 2020, 10:50 a.m. Cars on the road, not a kestrel to be seen on the outer camera and the nest is empty too – you can see it on the inner camera. Eleven viewers online. Two dislikes, sixty-four likes. I wish I could be up there myself, in the nest. On full-screen mode, I notice a tiny feather moving in the breeze.

26 March, 6:15 p.m. The sound is only working on the inner camera, but it's loud; I hear a train and then suddenly the kestrel. There it is on the outer camera, feathers puffed up in the loveliest light. The sunset casts a reddish glow on the glass facade of the office block. The train comes into view; who could be on it?

27 March, 9:12 a.m. Fresh out of the shower, I switch on both cameras. The kestrel is preening outside the nest – ruffling its feathers, picking at them with its beak. It looks right at me as if I'm disturbing it. Is it the female or the male? From where the bird is sitting, it can see my house. My doorbell rings; a TV crew is here to film me at home. I have to pretend

✳

For a few years now, I've been watching the kestrels as they brood their eggs in Zurich each summer atop the factory chimney on Josefstrasse and in other nest boxes installed by the city's Office of Parks and Open Spaces. I observe the young birds as they hatch, grow up and fledge. Or more accurately, I log in to the webcam live streams every now and then. Or to be really precise: the last few summers, I've occasionally glanced at a Twitter account that posts highlights from the kestrel cameras. But this spring I find myself checking the stream constantly, even keeping a kestrel diary, and sometimes following discussions about the Zurich birds on social media. Two cameras have been installed on the chimney: one inside the nest and one outside, giving wide views across the city. I envy these birds their vista, along with their power to spread their wings and fly away. I may live on the second floor, but I dwell on the ground, just like a field mouse, and my chief window on the world remains my MacBook Air.

---

to write, as if I'm watching the kestrels and noting down what I see. The falcon — or is it a tiercel? — is monitored day in, day out. Do we have the right? The camera is filming me from the front, but unlike the kestrel I'm not supposed to look into the lens as it comes across as unnatural. I smile to myself as I write these words down and that gets recorded too.

28 March, 11:15 a.m. Fourteen viewers outside, seven inside. Empty nest; white noise; the platform is covered in shit. Wrote to C about the TV crew and my birdwatching. He replied: *The TV crew came round to watch you watching a kestrel? And the kestrel itself watched from above as the TV people left your building and drove back to the studio afterwards. A vicious visual circle. But what if the kestrel has rigged the camera and the live images are only recordings? What if you think you're watching the kestrel, but the kestrel is really reading a book? One by Tom Kummer, at that?* My response: that's going straight in my kestrel diary.

29 March, Sunday. Didn't touch my computer. Spent the day thinking about my attempts to interpret my observations, to generate knowledge, and realised that I'm thinking more about the act of watching than about

Nonetheless, this gets me much closer to the kestrels than I ever could in nature. Of the many species of falcon across the world, three breed in Switzerland: the kestrel is distinguished by its fluttery hover, while the peregrine is harder to spot; it mainly makes itself known through the panic it sows among other birds. The third kind, the hobby, does not currently nest in Zurich.

And so I sit at my computer to watch these birds and I read books about them, especially the peregrine. I don't know if all falcons share the same breathtaking abilities, so what I am about to write applies solely to the peregrine – and even then I can provide only an inadequate account.

Humans can see twenty images per second, but falcons can see seventy to eighty; this high-speed resolution helps keep small prey in sight during even the most breakneck stoop. And yet falcons cannot see moving images on a screen. A falcon's eyesight is eight times sharper than a human's and when it focuses on something it obtains a crystal-clear image instantly: it can detect an insect

---

what I see the kestrels doing. I feel a little embarrassed about the TV show.

30 March. Cloudy weather; last night it snowed. Nobody home. The inner camera picks up noises that sound like steam trains. It makes me think of the TV series *Chernobyl*, which I finished watching yesterday.

31 March, 10:00 a.m. A slant of light falls on the nest. The falcon isn't here; nor is she at 12:15 p.m.

1 April 2020. The falcon is alone; the wind buffets her plumage enough to muss up her coiffure. It's 4:21 p.m.; nine people are watching her solitude.

2 April, 8:20 a.m. She's there, bathing in the light.

3 April, great excitement at 8:40 a.m.! Four kestrels are fluttering around the platform. All I can see is their wings – are they attacking the nest? Defending themselves? Mating? I know nothing whatsoever about these creatures.

4 April. Nobody home. Read the following in Helen MacDonald's *Falcon*: 'Is watching falcons on your computer monitor really watching falcons? Are falcon-cams simply soap operas in another guise, a nature-watching activity fit for an age of reality television?... Another symptom of the disappearance

measuring just one sixteenth of an inch from sixty feet away. To determine the size of and distance to its prey, the falcon bobs its head while keeping its eyes trained on the object of its desire. Humans refer to this ability as motion parallax.

In addition, the falcon — like all birds and certain other animals too — has four kinds of colour receptor in its eye, which means it can see ultraviolet light. The eyes of the female peregrine falcon (males are roughly a third smaller, hence the name tiercel) weigh around one ounce each. In human terms, a twelve-stone man with equivalent proportions would have eyes three inches in diameter that each weighed over four pounds.

The peregrine is the fastest animal on earth, reaching speeds of up to two hundred miles per hour when diving. Everything about this bird is built for the perfect fusion of keen eye and grasping claw. Or, as Helen Macdonald puts it: 'a falcon is a pair of eyes set in a well-armed, perfectly engineered airframe.'

Peregrines began to breed on the Josefstrasse chimney in

---

of animals from people's lives and their replacement with mere images, images framed by corporate symbolic investment?... Webcams allow a detailed familiarity with the lives of wild animals that previously only dedicated scientists, naturalists and hunters could obtain — with difficulty... These live-feed webcams, then, democratise natural knowledge.'

6 April, 2:00–3:00 p.m. The falcon hops in and out of the nest as if she's afraid. Later she preens; she can pivot her head 180 degrees like an owl. A second bird arrives, then both are gone.

7 April, 1:45 p.m. The falcon is looking out over the city. I briefly switch to the Altstetten camera, but the falcon above Josefswiese is closer to my heart. Then she's gone; all I hear is wind and birdsong. For a moment I'm not sure if the sounds are coming through the live feed or my open window.

8 April, 11:50 a.m. There are two of them! They whistle and screech — I don't know what to call it, I know too little of their language. Rather than just stare at the camera, I wish I could watch the kestrels in the flesh, find out where they hunt, whether they meet other kestrels on the way, whether they know each other, whether they're friends or enemies,

summer 2001. These birds love tradition, returning to the same nesting sites generation after generation; for hundreds of years they have settled on the same rocky bluffs as their forebears to raise their young.

My short-term interest is of little concern to the falcons; they nest and brood whether I am watching or not and their chicks fledge to return, hopefully, the following year.

Three years ago, a pair of kestrels went missing for several days on one of the Zurich web cameras, and so a warden had to rescue their young from the nesting box. He was able to retrieve four; two jumped off the platform, but were soon found again, and all six chicks were successfully raised at a raptor sanctuary. Yet no sooner had the young birds been dispatched to the rescue centre than the parents reappeared to find an empty nest.

Many falcons breed in Zurich, but for the last few years there have been no peregrines in the city. As natural predators, they also hunt domestic pigeons – and to settle the score, pigeon

whether they've also been stripping the shelves of flour and yeast like us humans. I don't know the first thing about them.

9 April, 5:50 p.m. No falcon, not a trace of her. These are long days now, they tumble through your fingers like sand. And while I can only watch my falcon via a camera, I read J. A. Baker's *The Peregrine* and learn how he pursued his falcon – how he clambered over gates, dashed across fields, cycled along paths. Yet he too was confined to the ground, like a field mouse. I don't know if that's a comforting thought but the mouse analogy appeals to me.

10 April, 9:40 a.m. The falcon is preening, but is startled by a noise and puffs her feathers up. Nothing else happens. I never see the falcon eat. She flies off. In Altstetten there are now three eggs, but none here.

11 April, Easter Saturday. Went on a bike ride. The entire Swiss Airlines fleet is grounded.

12 April, Easter Sunday. Only one plane in the sky, but no end of ducks.

13 April, 5:55 p.m. Twenty viewers online. The falcon is here. Phoned an ornithologist friend and watched the live stream with her; the first thing she

fanciers have deployed 'kamikaze birds' with poison smeared on their feathers. In one case, a peregrine who caught this deadly quarry died live on camera in front of its young on the Josefstrasse chimney, where kestrels now nest.

In his essay 'Why Birds Matter', Jonathan Franzen writes: 'If you could see every bird in the world, you'd see the whole world'. Birds live across the entire globe; just imagine if we could take in that full panorama, and if we had the vision of falcons.

---

noticed was all the tiny bones in the nest.

14 April, 11:45 a.m. The falcon is elsewhere. Re-read the two newspaper articles about how a peregrine was poisoned and died on-camera in the Josefstrasse nest some years ago, and how a clutch of kestrel chicks were prematurely 'rescued' when their parents briefly went missing.

15 April, 11:10 a.m. Fifty-five viewers. The falcon scratches her beard with her claw. She's calm today. Suddenly a second bird appears. I'm pretty sure these are two females, which I approve of. They haven't laid any eggs.

To watch the live feed, visit <https://www.stadt-zuerich.ch/ted/de/index/gsz/beratung-und-wissen/tier-und-mensch/falkenkamera.html>

BAR 63

IN ZURICH'S NIGHTLIFE DISTRICT, WHERE Rolandstrasse meets Zinistrasse, stands Bar 63. People from across the world live here, and there's a bar on every corner of the crossroads: Biondi to the right, Midway Bar and Catering Services to the left and Kaiser Franz across the way.

Bar 63 has an expensive mirror suspended at a slight angle over the counter so you can watch what's happening from above; a continual recitation of the moment.

At the foot of the mirror there are bottles arranged in rows: a shelf full of gin, and just below it, from every region on earth, the rum. They're sure to have what I need.

Winter's when I hanker after rum; in summer it's gin. The rain still feels cold but the evenings are growing brighter again. I am drawn to the heat of the tropics, locked up in the sweetness of the sugar cane. My rum comes with a square of rich, bitter chocolate.

I swirl this liquid sugar and set down the snifter, see my mirrored hands multiply in its bellied curve, resting on the many hands that have already held this glass, yesterday and the day before and the day before that; every one of us, they say, is linked by seven intersections.

The rum is sharp but sweet; in the muted light it gleams golden. How many people have toiled over this small measure? How many have cut and pressed and sold and distilled the sugar cane, have stored and bottled and shipped and finally brought it here and poured it for me into this short-stemmed, bulbous glass?

The music grows louder – *live from the garden* – grown man rap at its best. *Kumbaya bitch.*

My grandfather imported sugar cane, one of the first to do so, and joined forces with a dentist to fight the introduction of heavily refined crystalline sugar, writing letters to the Ministry of Health.

Looking at the globe, we see that sugar cane grows in a broad belt. Nestled above it is a narrower strip where juniper thrives: the Holarctic, extending from North America and southern Greenland to East Asia. More than seventeen bottles stand on the shelf; a monkey squats beneath a crown on the label of a brand of gin from the Black Forest. To prevent malaria, British East India Company soldiers were given quinine-rich tonic water to drink, with a dash of gin to make it less bitter. I cup my chin in my hands and rest my elbows on the bartop; solid wood, native oak, it fills almost half the room.

In the mirror, I see people come and go, smoking on the street or heading to Kaiser Franz. Biondi is only frequented by those who also go to pasta night at Midway Bar; the place is run by Cuban women with staff from Barbados and Antigua. Another world across the way.

I peel the foil from the chocolate and break a corner off as a cat hops onto the bar beside me, buries its little face in the bowl of peanuts and eats hastily, with loud crunches.

Before anyone can chase it away, the cat jumps off the counter and slinks through the humid music into the night. Later, after one or two more glasses, I step out into the thickening rain. The cat is now eating from a plate outside Midway Bar while a woman waits in the doorway studying the passers-by, who in turn stare into their miniature navigation devices. Then she stoops for the empty plate and takes it indoors as the cat shakes the water from its fur.

+SVIZRA is a series of eight chapbooks showcasing contemporary writing translated from the four official languages of Switzerland: German, French, Italian and Romansh. In giving equal visibility to each of the four languages, **+SVIZRA** offers a range of Swiss writing never before seen in English from a diverse group of some of the best authors living and working in Switzerland today, including National Literature Prize winning Anna Ruchat, Iraqi exile Usama Al-Shahmani and treasured Romansh author, Rut Plouda.

+SVIZRA is the result of Strangers Press' latest exciting collaboration with an international group of authors, translators, publishers, designers and editors, all made possible by generous funding from Pro Helvetia.

Supported By

University of East Anglia

NORWICH
UNIVERSITY
OF THE ARTS